To the real Delphi, with much

love, special girl ~ L G

For John, Laurie and James ~ P M

Copyright © 2006 by Good Books, Intercourse, PA 17534
International Standard Book Number: 1-56148-512-8
Library of Congress Catalog Card Number: 2005022188

Text copyright © Magi Publications 2006
Illustrations copyright © Patricia MacCarthy 2006

Original edition published in English by Little Tiger Press,
an imprint of Magi Publications, London, England, 2006.

Printed in Singapore by Tien Wah Press Pte.

Library of Congress Cataloging-in-Publication Data

Garnham, Laura.
The tiniest mermaid / by Laura Garnham and [illustrations by] Patricia MacCarthy.
p. cm.
Summary: Lily befriends an injured young mermaid, taking her home
to convalesce in an aquarium.
ISBN 1-56148-512-8 (hardcover)
[1. Mermaids--Fiction. 2. Friendship--Fiction.] I. MacCarthy, Patricia, ill. II. Title.

PZ7.G184374Tin 2006
[E]--dc22
2005022188

The Tiniest Mermaid

Laura Garnham

Illustrated by

Patricia MacCarthy

Good Books

Intercourse, PA 17534
800/762-7171
www.GoodBks.com

Lily lived by the wide blue sea.
On summer nights she would sit on
the beach, gazing out over the waves,
dreaming of magic and adventure.

One night, as she sat by the rock pools,
a faint sparkle caught her eye and a little
voice cried out, "Help! Please help me!"

Lily gasped. It was a mermaid!
A beautiful, tiny mermaid! Was
she dreaming? But the mermaid
called out again, "Help me,
please! My tail was hurt in
the storm last night and
I can't get back home!"

"Oh, you poor thing!" said Lily, kneeling
by the rock pool. "I'll help you, if I can."
"Thank you," whispered the mermaid.
"You'll be safe with me," said Lily softly.
"I'll look after you."

Lily scooped the
delicate mermaid
from the water.
She walked carefully
up the steps, through
the house to her room.
By her bed was a huge
glass fish tank, the perfect
place for a mermaid to rest.
As she slipped into the water the tiny mermaid smiled.
"I'm Delphi. What's your name?"
"Lily," said Lily, smiling back at her new friend.

That night Lily sat up for a long time, watching over Delphi
as she slept. "I just knew mermaids were real," she whispered
to the fish. "Now you let her sleep and get better."

The next morning Lily leaped out of bed and rushed to the fish tank. Had it all been a dream? She stared anxiously through the glass and there, in the castle, was Delphi!

"You're still here!" Lily cried with delight.

"Of course," laughed Delphi. "Where else would I be?"

Delphi was looking much better, and Lily saw that her tail was twinkling gently. She thought she had never seen anything so beautiful in all her life.

Lily and Delphi talked all day. Delphi spoke of a world where mermaids swam through the coral, playing with sea horses. Lily could almost feel the water and see the light and color of the ocean.

That night her dreams were filled with magic and mermaids and a special place far, far under the sea.

Slowly Delphi grew stronger. As her magic returned her tail sparkled brighter, and she transformed the tank into a shimmering underwater wonderland.

Lily raced home after school each day, and she and Delphi talked and talked until they were the best of friends.

"I wish I was a mermaid," said Lily one night.

"It is wonderful," Delphi said wistfully. "My friends and I travel the whole world helping trapped or hurt animals. And sometimes we use our sparkling tails to guide sailors home through terrible storms."

"Wow!" said Lily in wonder. "I never knew!"

"It's exciting, but it can be very scary," said Delphi. "When I was hurt in that awful storm, I was separated from my friends by a huge wave and thrown onto the rocks." She sighed. "They must be wondering what happened to me."

Lily gasped. Delphi's friends would be worried about her.

"Oh, Delphi," she cried. "You must go back to your friends!"

"Yes, I must," said Delphi. "But I shall miss you."

"If only we didn't have to say good-bye!" sighed Lily. "I wish I could come with you. Or just visit your magical world."

Delphi smiled suddenly. "I could show you, if you like. Close your eyes . . ."

Lily took a deep breath as Delphi started singing a gentle, lilting song. Lily could feel magic all round her and hear the rush of the ocean growing louder . . .

All at once she was there with Delphi, swimming with dolphins as they danced and dived through the water.
Further and further they swam through the warm blue ocean until the setting sun turned the white beaches gold.

When Lily fell asleep that night she could still hear the whale's song and feel the sand between her toes.

The next morning Lily cradled Delphi in her hands
for the very last time as she carried her to the seashore.
  "Don't be sad, Lily," said Delphi softly, and she gave
her a special shell. "Whenever you miss me," she said,
"put the shell to your ear and you will hear the magic
of the sea whispering inside."

With a flick of her glittering tail, the tiny mermaid
swam off. But as she waved good-bye, Lily saw two more
shining tails appear at Delphi's side. Delphi was with her
friends, and she was safe. And Lily knew that whenever
she missed her, she could listen to the sounds of the
shell and look for the sparkles glimmering in the sea,
for Delphi would always be near.